Kits, Cubs, and Calves

An Arctic Summer

In memory of Uncle James and Andrea, and
everyone named Akittiq after her.

Published by Inhabit Media Inc.
www.inhabitmedia.com

Inhabit Media Inc. (Iqaluit) P.O. Box 11125, Iqaluit, Nunavut, X0A 1H0
(Toronto) 191 Eglinton Avenue East, Suite 310, Toronto, Ontario, M4P 1K1

Editors: Neil Christopher and Kelly Ward
Art Director: Danny Christopher

This project was made possible in part by the Government of Canada.

We acknowledge the support of the Canada Council for the Arts for our publishing program.

Library and Archives Canada Cataloguing in Publication

Title: Kits, cubs, and calves : an Arctic summer / by Suzie Napayok-Short ; illustrated by Tamara
    Campeau.
Names: Napayok-Short, Suzie, author. | Campeau, Tamara, illustrator.
Identifiers: Canadiana 20200244116 | ISBN 9781772272741 (hardcover)
Subjects: LCSH: Tundra animals—Infancy—Arctic regions—Juvenile literature. | LCSH: Parental
    behavior in animals—Arctic regions—Juvenile literature. | LCSH: Familial behavior in animals—
    Arctic regions—Juvenile literature.
Classification: LCC QL105 .N37 2020 | DDC j591.75/86—dc23

Printed in Canada

Kits, Cubs, and Calves
An Arctic Summer

by Suzie Napayok-Short

illustrated by Tamara Campeau

Akuluk has been visiting her *anaana* and *ataata*, her names for her grandma and grandpa, in their small community in Nunavut. She travelled to visit her family all on her own from her home south of the Arctic. But it's now time to go. Akuluk is off to another community to visit her uncle James and aunt Sulie. She climbs into a noisy, northern float plane all dressed up in her *atigi*, a red duffle parka with a large fur trim called a sunburst. Akuluk is ready for a trip into the blue, Arctic sky.

An hour later, the bush pilots land the plane on the water. It glides smoothly toward the shore. Akuluk, holding tightly onto her stuffed polar bear, Piulua, steps down onto the dock to meet Uncle James.

"Welcome to Saattut, Akuluk. I think you'll have fun while you're here!" Uncle James says. Saattut means "the flatlands," and it is the name of the community where Akuluk's uncle James and aunt Sulie live.

After putting her bags in the back, they ride down the gravel road in Uncle James's white truck. Along the way, Akuluk sees a brownish-red fox with her kits playing on the tundra.

3

Stopping outside their house, Aunt Sulie explains that their dog Blackie had puppies last month. Seven of them are running around.

"You are welcome to say hello to them!" Aunt Sulie says.

The puppies are happy and excited to see someone new. One clumsily runs to Akuluk, and the rest follow behind. The puppies, bouncing on and off of Akuluk's legs, all jump and wag their fluffy black-and-white tails. Akuluk moves toward a puppy with dots above his eyes and massive paws. She can clearly tell he will be the lead dog of this team.

"You're the boss, pup!" Akuluk says, imagining the puppy pulling a *qamutiik*, the sled Inuit use to travel across the ice and snow. "I just know you'll be the leader when you grow up."

Akuluk laughs as she cuddles with the playful pup, who nips gently at her. Blackie watches carefully to make sure her pups are safe.

5

Inside, Aunt Sulie shows Akuluk her room.

"Make yourself comfortable here tonight," Aunt Sulie says, "and we shall head off tomorrow morning to check on our old camping grounds. It seems we can't camp there anymore. The polar bears have taken over our island! We'll get just close enough for your uncle James to take some pictures."

How exciting! Akuluk thinks. A million questions bubble out of her. "Polar bears? Like real polar bears? Are they big? And aren't they scary? What if they're really hungry?" Akuluk has lots of thoughts racing through her mind.

"I think we'll bring an underwater sound recorder, too, in case we see some seals or whales," Uncle James says.

"Wow! Really?" Akuluk is surprised. "An underwater sound recorder? Where did you get one all the way up here, Uncle James? That is awesome!"

"Well, I ordered it online, actually. And believe it or not, we do use computers here in Saattut, too." Uncle James chuckles as he teases Akuluk.

The next morning, Aunt Sulie prepares some dried Arctic char while Akuluk packs the *palaugaaq*, bannock, and *aqpiit*, orange cloudberries, that her grandma had stuffed in her knapsack. They will eat on the boat on the way back from the camping grounds. Uncle Tommy will be coming, too.

The sun shines brightly on Akuluk's face, even though it is very early. The sun is up twenty-four hours a day here! Uncle Tommy drives everyone to the shore.

Parking the truck, he lifts Akuluk, with Piulua under her arm, over the side of the boat. With everyone on board, he backs the trailer into the salty Arctic Ocean. *Vroom*! The twin engines come to life and they're off, splashing from wave to wave, with the whistling wind pulling at Akuluk's curly black hair.

As they cruise out into the open ocean, Uncle Tommy spots beluga whales in a pod, all swimming together. He points them out to Uncle James.

"Whoa, lets ease down a bit here, Tommy," Uncle James instructs. "We don't want to hit any of these beautiful animals."

Sulie, Akuluk, and Piulua are all hushed in amazement at seeing this pod of whales in the sea. They are creamy white and look like they have big, happy smiles.

One large, white beluga surfacing among the waves actually has a little grey calf with her! Akuluk's eyes open wide as she holds onto the boat and Piulua at the same time. Akuluk has never seen anything like this before. Belugas—even a baby—swimming playfully and freely in the icy waters of their Arctic home.

Tommy carefully slows the boat, and Uncle James slips his recording device into the ocean to hear the whales' sounds.

Akuluk listens carefully with the headphones Uncle Tommy hands her. She can hear the mother beluga making cooing sounds, sometimes clicking, then chattering and whistling. Sometimes she makes very low sounds to her baby that remind Akuluk of the deep sounds of throat singers she heard during her last trip to Nunavut. Akuluk is on her second trip up north and still doesn't know much of her mother's language yet. She asks Aunt Sulie what the word for "small" is in Inuktitut. Aunt Sulie replies, "*mikilaaq*." It means "littlest one."

Akuluk asks, "Is it okay for me to name the baby 'Miki'?"

Aunt Sulie says that would be great, and easier for Akuluk to say, too.

With his listening device, Uncle James follows the mother and the little *qinalugaq*, the Inuktitut word for "beluga whale," in the deep, dark water. They all listen to the sounds the whales make. Miki squeals with delight, sounding much like a human baby, whenever he gets excited and joyful. He flaps his little tail to make a big splash before heading down beneath his mother, who is floating on the surface.

Aunt Sulie explains that in the *piusituqait*, the traditional ways, of the whales, they have always looked after one another. "They swim and feed in the mighty Arctic Ocean, talking constantly with whistles, coos, chatters, clicks, and throat songs, keeping track of one another that way."

Akuluk thinks, *Wow! They communicate almost the same way Inuit do.* The little whale slides beneath his mother, then surfaces again to breathe with her. With Miki safely beside her, the mother beluga dives deep below the surface and makes huge bubble rings that float to the top of the water. Then she soars upward and—*slosh*— lands on the surface with a great big splash. She then dives silently back below the surface. Together, Miki and her mother dance and flow gracefully in perfect harmony.

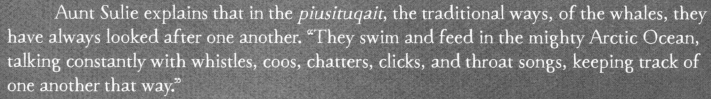

Akuluk sees seagulls and Arctic terns bobbing up and down in the air, making loud noises above her. She is surprised to see something grey on the surface of the water, floating toward them. Akuluk begins to wonder. *What could that be? Maybe a polar bear cub?* As if reading her mind, Aunt Sulie says with surprise, "Oh, look at that chubby, round, and very tiny whale swimming all by itself."

The little grey one swims toward the pod, stopping often along the way to breathe. It seems at times to have trouble moving forward. The mother beluga soon spots the calf, and after a moment she begins moving cautiously toward the little whale. She swims around it, as if wondering why it's alone, checking to see if it's okay. Akuluk is thrilled to hear the sounds of the mother whale and the lone baby in the water. She watches the other whales taking turns checking the newcomer quietly, filled with their own curiosity. The mother's sounds become slow and low. Then suddenly, they change to very fast clicking noises. The little orphan whale barely makes any noise.

    Where did it come from? Akuluk thinks. Akuluk can hear the seagulls screeching above. They see the baby whale on top of the water, too.

The boat is getting close to shore. Above Akuluk's head, several gulls fly together, chattering loudly. They watch the people in the boat below them, who in turn watch the whales in the water. Uncle Tommy explains that sometimes beluga whales adopt orphans, just like human beings do.

"We will have to watch carefully to see what this beluga will do, as she has one baby already," Uncle Tommy says. "Belugas have a tendency to help one another out, and they have younger female belugas that look after the smaller ones in their pod."

Hearing this, Akuluk hopes the mother beluga will decide to adopt the tiny, grey whale. The other whales have surrounded the mother, waiting for her to decide. Everyone it seems—human and animal— hopes the orphan won't end up alone or be left behind.

Uncle James is suddenly excited.

"Look at the old camping grounds over there, Akuluk," he says. "See the *nanuit*, the polar bears? They're close to the shore."

Uncle James explains that these bears have made this old camp their own since they found fishing nets filled with char that the family used to set up for themselves at the camp. They have come back every year since, so the family has had to give up their traditional land to help these large animals survive.

"We decided to let them be," Uncle James tells Akuluk. "We will have to find another place for ourselves."

Akuluk sees the biggest and the grandest *nanuq*, the strongest and the toughest animal in the Arctic, eating a catch of seal meat. One of her cubs is on the ground nearby, napping on and off. The mother hears the noise of the boat and turns to look, then turns back to lick her cubs' faces as if to say, "You stay here." The cubs watch their mother's movements.

"The cubs are used to moving quickly if people get too close to them," says Uncle Tommy.

Uncle James tells Tommy to cut the engine. He doesn't want bears swimming in the water where they will see the belugas with their calves and hunt them. That could happen quickly, and nanuq is powerful at hunting whales in the water.

The mother bear hardly pays them any notice, now that she sees how far away the boat really is. Polar bears are very good at determining distances.

Uncle Tommy points at the seal meat by the bear and says, "She has plenty of food for now. Maybe for us, that is a very good thing!"

There are countless seagulls and Arctic terns on the island with the bears. Uncle James explains that at this time of year, during the summer, the seagulls stay close to the mother bear while she eats, hoping to catch a snippet of meat. "The Arctic foxes are gone, and it's the seagulls' turn to follow nanuq," Uncle James says.

In the winter, the foxes follow nanuq everywhere, eating the meat the bears leave behind. Uncle James tells everyone that in the summer, the foxes' fur turns a beautiful orangey, brownish-red colour, matching the rocks and heather, and making it very hard to see them. They have kits in their dens during this time, too. Nanuq will take those kits away from their mother and feed on them with her cubs, so the foxes know to stay away. The seagulls come around in the early spring and replace the foxes as nanuq's followers for the season. When the kits get bigger, their mother will take them out of the den and onto the tundra.

Akuluk remembers the mother fox and her kits that she and Piulua saw as they drove into town the day before.

"Why don't nanuit chase after caribou?" Akuluk asks. "There are so many around."

Uncle Tommy explains that caribou are far too fast for nanuq.

"Caribou mostly stay farther inland, away from the coast, until their calves are old enough to walk with their mothers to the shore for the cooler winds they need that come off the sea. The land can get very hot in the summer," Uncle Tommy explains.

"Nanuq likes the ocean and the shore, where he can find seals," Uncle James adds. "He hunts belugas, too."

As they pull away from the shore, Akuluk stands with Aunt Sulie and watches the belugas.

The mother beluga is still floating close to the lone calf. She treats it like a lost child, seeming to ask for it to stay close, checking to see if it will follow her when she turns. It does.

"She has accepted the newcomer into her family," Aunt Sulie says with a smile.

All the whales in the pod appear happy with the decision, too. The mother, Miki, and the orphan all swim together. Miki, who has a new playmate and friend, happily and noisily splashes his back flippers as if to say to the boat, "*Tagvauvusi*! Farewell!" The pod of belugas is leaving.

As they watch the whales swim off, Aunt Sulie turns to Akuluk. "Everywhere we go, Inuit and animals, we all have a need to stay close, so we can help one another," she says, putting an arm around Akuluk. "The wildlife do what they can to help one another, in their own way, and we do what we can in ours. We have to share our earth with all the wildlife that live here. We need to look after our land, and the plants in it, too."

Akuluk thinks about what Aunt Sulie has said as she watches the belugas swimming off into the distance, the little orphan safely surrounded by his new family.

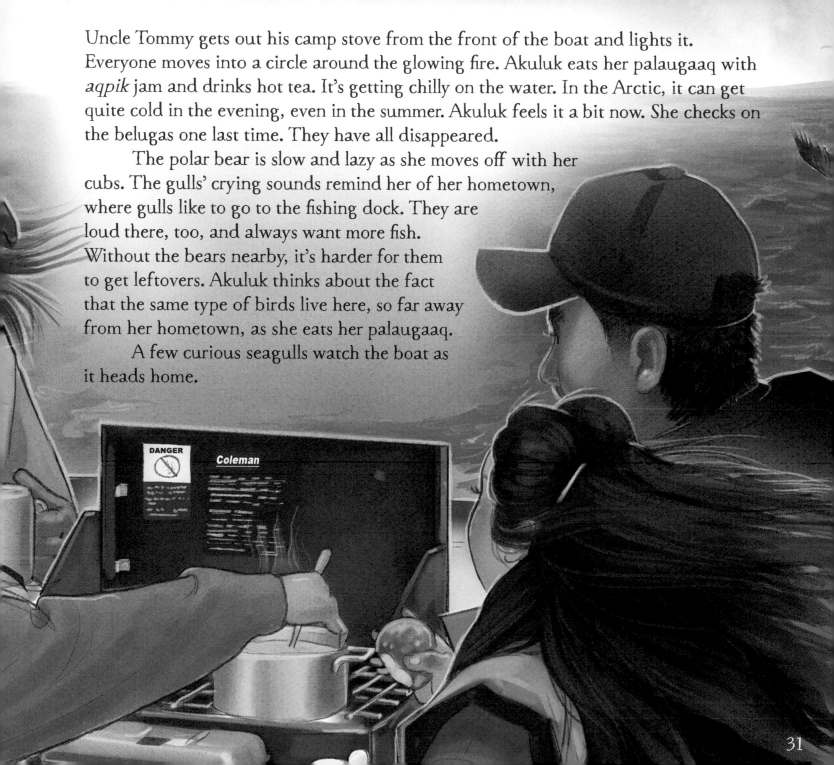

Uncle Tommy gets out his camp stove from the front of the boat and lights it. Everyone moves into a circle around the glowing fire. Akuluk eats her palaugaaq with *aqpik* jam and drinks hot tea. It's getting chilly on the water. In the Arctic, it can get quite cold in the evening, even in the summer. Akuluk feels it a bit now. She checks on the belugas one last time. They have all disappeared.

The polar bear is slow and lazy as she moves off with her cubs. The gulls' crying sounds remind her of her hometown, where gulls like to go to the fishing dock. They are loud there, too, and always want more fish. Without the bears nearby, it's harder for them to get leftovers. Akuluk thinks about the fact that the same type of birds live here, so far away from her hometown, as she eats her palaugaaq.

A few curious seagulls watch the boat as it heads home.

Back in her room, Akuluk finds a stuffed white beluga whale sitting on her pillow. What a wonderful way to remember this trip!

"Thank you, Uncle James and Aunt Sulie! I am going to call him 'Miki,'" Akuluk says, as she settles into bed with Miki and Piulua.

As she drifts off to sleep, Akuluk thinks of all the polar bears, belugas, and foxes, and the seagulls with their squawking cries. Closing her eyes, she dreams about dancing with waddling bears and swimming with baby belugas in the great Arctic sea.

Notes on Inuktitut Pronunciation

There are some sounds in Inuktitut that may be unfamiliar to English speakers. The pronunciations below convey those sounds in the following ways:

• A double vowel (e.g., aa, ee) lengthens the vowel sound.

• Capitalized letters denote the emphasis for each word.

• **q** is a "uvular" sound, a sound that comes from the very back of the throat. This is distinct from the sound for k, which is the same as a typical English "k" sound (known as a "velar" sound).

For more Inuktitut resources, visit inhabitmedia.com/inuitnipingit

Akuluk (pronounced AAH-ko-look) name meaning "the loved one"

anaana (pronounced a-NAA-na) mother of Akuluk's mom, thus grandmother to Akuluk

aqpiit (pronounced AQ-peet) cloudberries, sometimes called the "orange raspberries of the North"

aqpik (pronounced AQ-pik) one cloudberry

ataata (pronounced a-TAA-ta) father of Akuluk's mom, thus grandfather to Akuluk

atigi (pronounced a-TI-gi) coat or parka

Mikilaaq (pronounced mi-ki-LAAQ) name meaning "the smallest one"

nanuit (pronounced na-no-EET) polar bears

nanuq (pronounced na-NOOQ) one polar bear

palaugaaq (pronounced pa-la-oo-GAAQ) bannock, a delicious biscuit bread

Piulua (pronounced PEW-lo-ah) name meaning "the most beautiful"

piusituqait (pronounced PEW-si-tu-qa-it) traditional or customary ways

qamutiik (pronounced qa-mu-TEEK) traditional travel sled used by Inuit

qinalugaq (pronounced qi-na-lu-GAQ) beluga whale

Saattut (pronounced SAA-toot) A place name that means "flat lands"

Tagvauvusi! (pronounced tag-va-OO-vu-si!) Farewell!

Suzie Napayok-Short was born in Frobisher Bay and grew up in Apex and Foxe Main on Baffin Island. She eventually moved to Coral Harbour, Nunavut, and later to Iqaluit, Nunavut. Suzie built a career as an Inuktitut translator and interpreter working across Nunavut, and the Northwest Territories and throughout Canada. Suzie currently lives in Yellowknife, Northwest Territories, with her husband. Suzie writes articles for magazines such as *The Walrus, Tusaajaksat, and Arctic Policy,* among others. Her article "Words from Whale Cove," published in *The Walrus,* was nominated for a 2020 National Magazine Award. She runs the website Inuit Creative Products, which helps artists and crafters with sales. Suzie's first book for children, *Wild Eggs: A Tale of Arctic Egg Collecting,* was nominated for the Silver Birch Express Award.

Tamara Campeau's illustration journey began at Dawson College, where she earned her associate degree in illustration and design. Shortly after, she furthered her studies at Sheridan College, where she obtained her bachelor's degree in illustration with honours. Tamara works digitally to bring stories to life through her painterly illustrations. Her work has a strong sense of lighting and vibrant colour palettes, along with dynamic compositions. She loves creating endearing characters with a strong sense of personality and emotion. Her work is inspired by wildlife, children, and the environments they reside in. She uses this inspiration to add a layer of realism to her illustrations. When she's not at her desk, she can be found breaking a sweat at the local gym or exploring nature with her standard poodle, Peanut.

Inhabit Media Inc.
www.inhabitmedia.com